Library of Congress Control Number: 2023937115

ISBN 978-0-06-325173-1

The artist used watercolor, pencil, acrylic, colored pencil, and
pretty much everything else under the sun, including an
iMac, to create the digital illustrations for this book.

Typography by Chelsea C. Donaldson

23 24 25 25 27  RTLO  10 9 8 7 6 5 4 3 2 1

First Edition

*For the wildlife conservationists who fight tirelessly for all earth's
creatures, giving voices to the voiceless, and inspiring the next
generation to care about every species living on planet Earth —B.F.*

*For Andie and Harrison —B.W.*

# SOLAR BEAR

*words by* Beth Ferry    *pictures by* Brendan Wenzel

HARPER

*An Imprint of HarperCollinsPublishers*

I am a mighty solar bear.
No ordinary polar bear.
'Cause I can shine and I can glow,
brighter than the whitest snow.

Today I leave my arctic pole
to start a solar bear patrol.
With bears from south and bears from north,
together we will venture forth
to tell a tale that's hard to hear,
to tell it while we still are here,
before we all just . . . disappear.

Our light will shine on what is wrong.

On disappearing orca's song.

On ivory tusks.

And rhino's horn.

On tiny turtles not yet born.

On otters, sloths, and manatees.

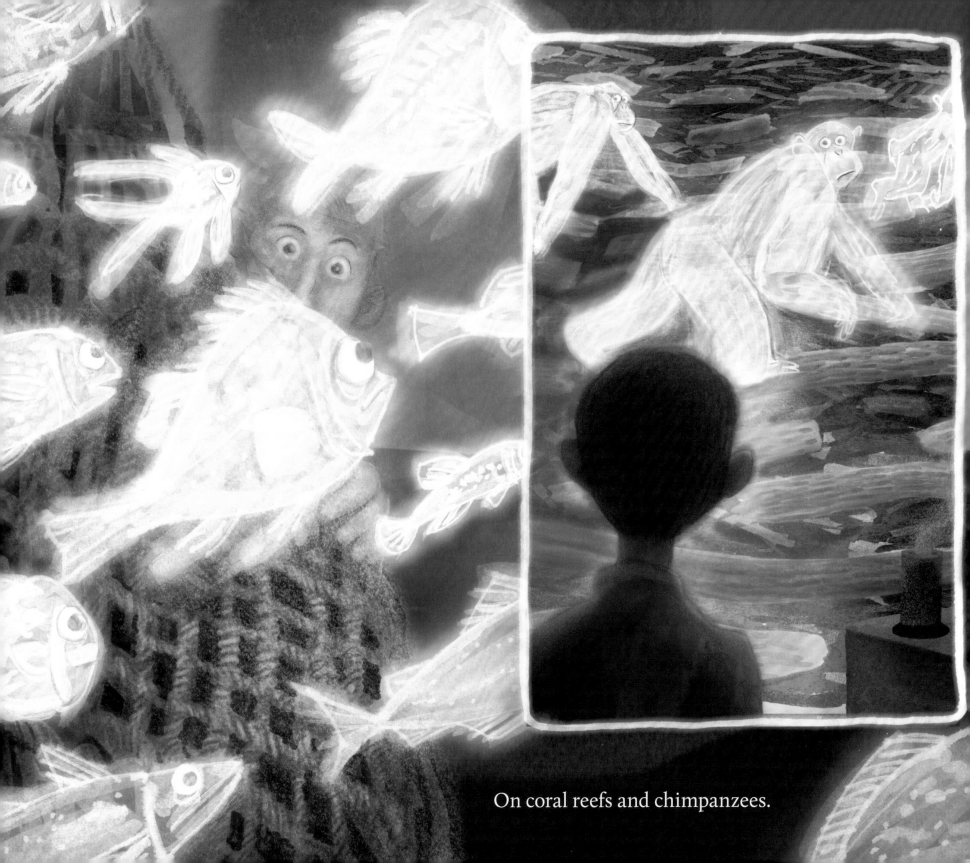

On coral reefs and chimpanzees.

On pangolins with pinecone scales.

Orangutans and humpback whales

On bees and trees and butterflies.
On living things of every size.

Our light will be a lion's roar,
too loud for you to just ignore.
From those of us who have no voice
to those of you who have a choice.

We'll show you that our paths are linked—
as you expand, we go extinct.

We'll shine so brightly that you'll see
that change is a necessity.

We'll walk the plains
    and run the beaches,
        travel to the out-of-reaches.

Warm you with our solar light.

Try to show you what is right.

We'll tell you that the words *Who cares?* are killing all the polar bears.

We'll come to meet each of your friends

to tell you how the story ends.

To show you how the future looks
when creatures live nowhere but books.

We'll ask you for your mighty roar
to show us we're worth fighting for
so we won't worry anymore.

We cannot fight this fight alone.
We cannot do it on our own.

The earth is ours.
Yours and mine.
So dare to care.
To glow. To shine.
'Cause if you would,
and when you did,

then you will be a solar kid.

And you will change the world, I know.

And I can rest, safe in the snow.

This book mentions only a few animals that are endangered or critically endangered. However, there are thousands more that need our help and deserve our attention.

## HOW MANY SPECIES ARE THERE?

No one knows for sure! It is estimated that there are 8.7 million known species on earth—6.5 million on land and 2.2 million in the ocean. But this is a huge underestimation. Humans don't have the resources necessary to find and study every species on earth. Remember, the word *species* includes animals (mammals, fish, reptiles, birds, and amphibians), insects, plants, and corals. When a new species is discovered, it is usually an insect.

The most famous endangered species are called **Charismatic Megafauna**. These include the giant panda, the tiger, the blue whale, the gorilla, the snow leopard, and the Asian elephant. They are called this because they are big and beautiful and draw much more attention than the sea marigold or the king rat, who are just as endangered.

**The International Union for the Conservation of Nature** compiles a list—called the Red List—of all threatened species, including corals, birds, mammals, insects, and plants. It is estimated that over 37,000 species are endangered and at risk of extinction. Be aware that this number is out of the approximately 79,000 species that have been assessed. The IUCN is working to evaluate as many species as possible.

**The leading causes of extinction** are results of human activity. It is estimated that current extinction rates are up to 1,000 times higher than they would have been without humans. Activities that endanger plants and wildlife include:

- HABITAT DESTRUCTION AND FRAGMENTATION
- POLLUTION
- CLIMATE CHANGE
- OVERPOPULATION
- POACHING AND HUNTING

## HOW CAN YOU BECOME A SOLAR KID?

Be informed! Learn as much as you can about what is happening to the animals of planet Earth. Recycle. Carpool. Plant a tree. Reuse paper. Pick up trash when you see it. Use sustainable products. Never buy ivory. Build a bee hotel. Conserve water and electricity. Use renewable energy. Ask your guardians about solar panels. Learn about climate change. Share your knowledge with your family, friends, and teachers. Remember—your voice matters!

**Roots and Shoots** is a humanitarian and environmental program where you can learn about how to make a difference and become an agent for change and a solar kid. www.rootsandshoots.org

# THERE ARE WONDERFUL SUCCESS STORIES THAT TELL US WHAT WE DO MATTERS

In 2016, the **giant panda** was moved off the endangered species list and on to the vulnerable list by the IUCN. The panda had been considered endangered for many decades, due mainly to habitat loss. Conservation efforts in China have led to this success.

In 1996, the **black-footed ferret** was considered extinct in the wild, but captive breeding helped the species to recover, and the ferrets were reintroduced to the wild in 2012. They are still one of North America's most endangered mammals as a result of habitat loss and non-native disease.

The **bald eagle** population in North America was labeled endangered in 1963. Loss of habitat, hunting, and pesticides were contributing to the decline in population. DDT, a pesticide used to kill weeds, entered the water system and contaminated the fish that eagles ate. The chemical interfered with the eagles' ability to produce strong eggshells, and baby eaglets could not hatch. This also affected **peregrine falcons** and **brown pelicans**. With help from the government—which included captive breeding, nesting site protections, and restrictions on DDT—the bald eagle was removed from the endangered species list in 2007.

The **humpback whale** was listed as critically endangered in 1970. Regulations on the hunting and killing of whales imposed by the International Whaling Commission have been successful. Since 2016, nine of the fourteen distinct humpback populations have been taken off the endangered species list, although they will still be protected.

## RESOURCES

**The International Union for the Conservation of Nature's Red List of Threatened Species (IUCN)**
www.iucnredlist.org

**Polar Bears International**
www.polarbearsinternational.com

**The National Wildlife Federation**
www.nwf.org

**The U.S. Fish and Wildlife Service and the Endangered Species Act**
www.fws.gov/program/endangered-species

*Hope for Animals and Their World: How Endangered Species Are Being Rescued from the Brink* by Jane Goodall

## AUTHOR'S NOTE

This book was inspired by an image I saw of an exhausted polar bear swimming in the sea, searching for a place to rest with no land or ice in sight. I read the article attached to the image, which detailed the crisis polar bears are facing due to melting arctic ice. The melting ice is caused by climate change, which is caused by human activity. I was struck by this in such a visceral way that I began to research endangered species and realized the polar bear crisis was just the tip of the iceberg. What I read saddened me but, more importantly, inspired me to call attention to the powerful impact human actions and decisions have on nature and the necessity to change the future. Who better to change the future than you?

## ILLUSTRATOR'S NOTE

In 2009 a poacher's bullet ended the life of the last Vietnamese rhinoceros. In the blink of an eye, an extraordinary subspecies, which had wallowed through the muddy forests of Southeast Asia for millennia, vanished forever. I lived in Vietnam at the time and had slept one hundred miles away from where the great gray wonder fell. It shook me to my core. I knew animals went extinct, but I somehow believed extinction only happened long ago. How could humans, with all our power and ability, have let this occur?

The heartbreaking event motivated me to learn more, and the more I read and traveled, the clearer it became that even in the wildest places, the human world posed a threat to nature, pushing the rest of life to the edges of the map—or in the case of the Vietnamese rhinoceros, and too many others, off it completely.

Connecting with wildlife conservationists—inspiring humans who worked day and night to protect wild creatures and places—gave me new hope. Their vision of what this wondrous planet could be if treated with respect has helped me imagine a better world. What if flocks of colorful birds filled the skies each season, countless whales breached just off our beaches, and muddy rhinoceroses happily wallowed just past the edges of our cities? What would it feel like to live in a world like that? We have the power to bring such a place to be. The information in the back of this book explores some great ways to start down that path. I hope you will continue down it with curiosity and an open heart. Who knows the extraordinary places it may lead us all?